CW00349708

CONT...

Published by Pedigree Books Limited
Beech Hill House, Walnut Gardens, Exeter, Devon EX4 4DH. Published 2009.

SINNOH STICKERS

These profiles need personalising! Read the descriptions, work out who's who and then bring the pages to life with the right names and character stickers. You'll also find a quick quiz to keep you on your toes!

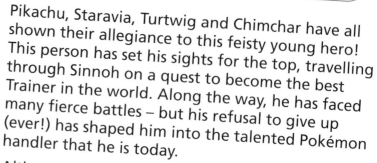

Pikachu, Staravia, Turtwig and Chimchar have all shown their allegiance to this feisty young hero! This person has set his sights for the top, travelling through Sinnoh on a quest to become the best Trainer in the world. Along the way, he has faced many fierce battles – but his refusal to give up (ever!) has shaped him into the talented Pokémon handler that he is today.

Although he can be rash and over-excited at times, this person always treats his Pokémon with kindness and respect. As a result Pikachu has become an exceptionally devoted friend and loyal follower. When Team Rocket try to get their hands on the Electric Pokémon, this person proves time and again that he will do anything to get Pikachu back.

QUICK TRIV

1. Where was this Trainer born?

_____

2. What is this person's surname?

_____

3. Which competitive young Trainer has become Ash's rival?

_____

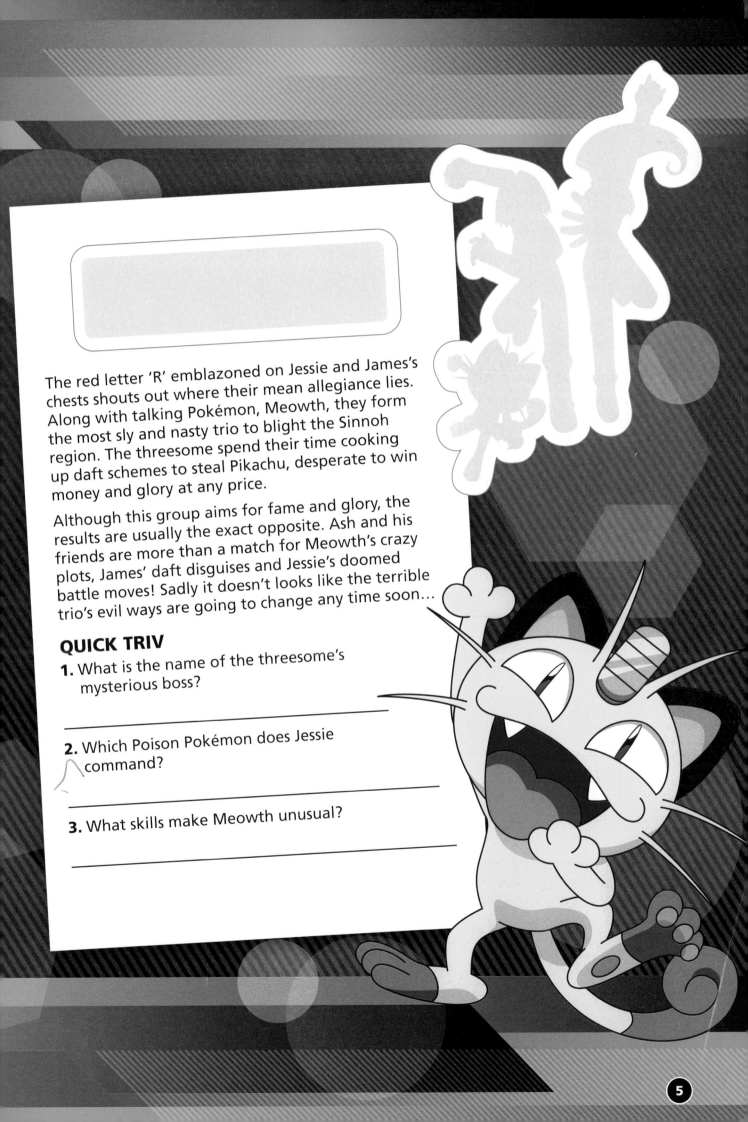

The red letter 'R' emblazoned on Jessie and James's chests shouts out where their mean allegiance lies. Along with talking Pokémon, Meowth, they form the most sly and nasty trio to blight the Sinnoh region. The threesome spend their time cooking up daft schemes to steal Pikachu, desperate to win money and glory at any price.

Although this group aims for fame and glory, the results are usually the exact opposite. Ash and his friends are more than a match for Meowth's crazy plots, James' daft disguises and Jessie's doomed battle moves! Sadly it doesn't looks like the terrible trio's evil ways are going to change any time soon…

QUICK TRIV

1. What is the name of the threesome's mysterious boss?

_____

2. Which Poison Pokémon does Jessie command?

_____

3. What skills make Meowth unusual?

_____

SINNOH STICKERS

This person is both Ash's longest travelling companion and wisest friend. The ex-Gym leader likes to keeps an eye out for the Trainer, making sure that he's always on hand to suggest Battle tactics and new moves. It seems that nothing can phase this guy, apart from the arrival of a pretty girl!

As well as being a talented Breeder, this person knows just the right way to calm and care for troubled Pokémon. He is able to whip up a delicious meal for any type at a moment's notice and shows great skill in interpreting Pokémon behaviour. When he took first prize in the Pokémon Dress-up Contest, this person was thrilled to win a Happiny egg.

QUICK TRIV

1. Which Gym did this Breeder once lead?

_____

2. Which Pokémon can be counted on to drag this guy away from the ladies?

_____

3. What is the person's favourite hobby?

_____

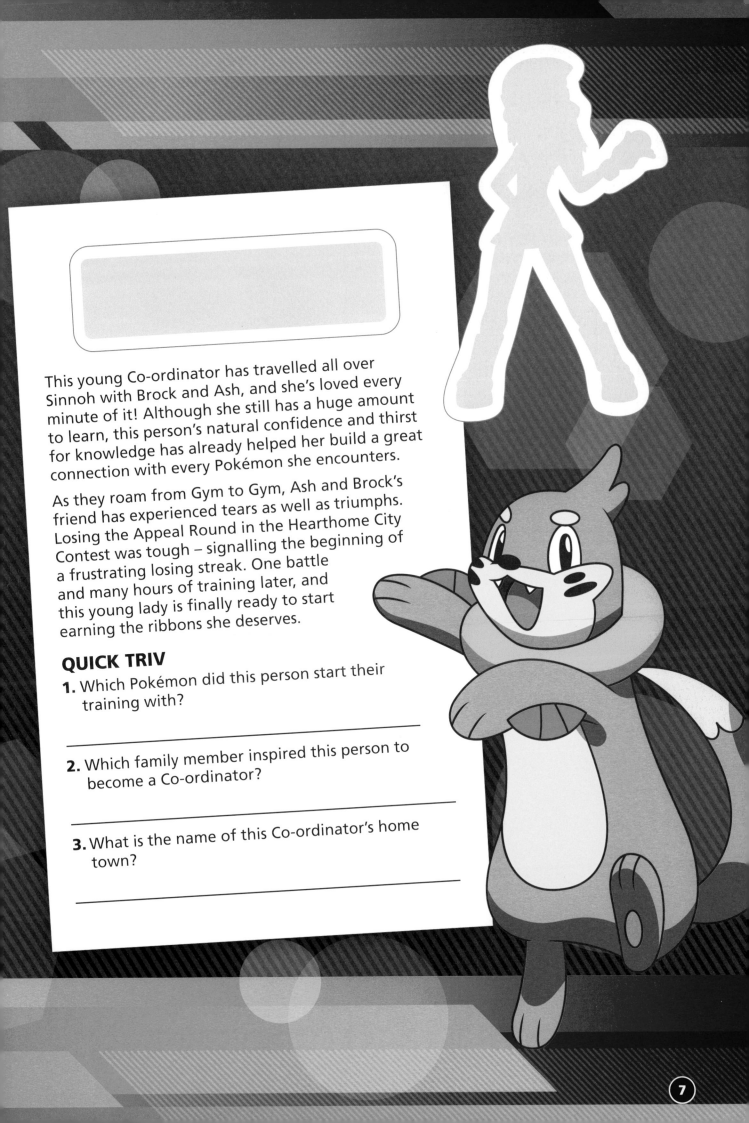

This young Co-ordinator has travelled all over Sinnoh with Brock and Ash, and she's loved every minute of it! Although she still has a huge amount to learn, this person's natural confidence and thirst for knowledge has already helped her build a great connection with every Pokémon she encounters.

As they roam from Gym to Gym, Ash and Brock's friend has experienced tears as well as triumphs. Losing the Appeal Round in the Hearthome City Contest was tough – signalling the beginning of a frustrating losing streak. One battle and many hours of training later, and this young lady is finally ready to start earning the ribbons she deserves.

QUICK TRIV

1. Which Pokémon did this person start their training with?

_____

2. Which family member inspired this person to become a Co-ordinator?

_____

3. What is the name of this Co-ordinator's home town?

_____

CRESSELIA COLOUR COPY GRID

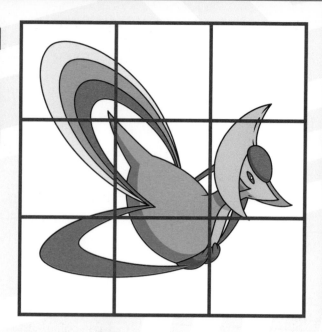

Can you draw this curious Psychic Pokémon? Cressalia releases glistening particles from its orb-shaped wings, soothing sleepers and banishing nightmares. Copy each picture square into the big grid below, then use felt-tips to colour it in!

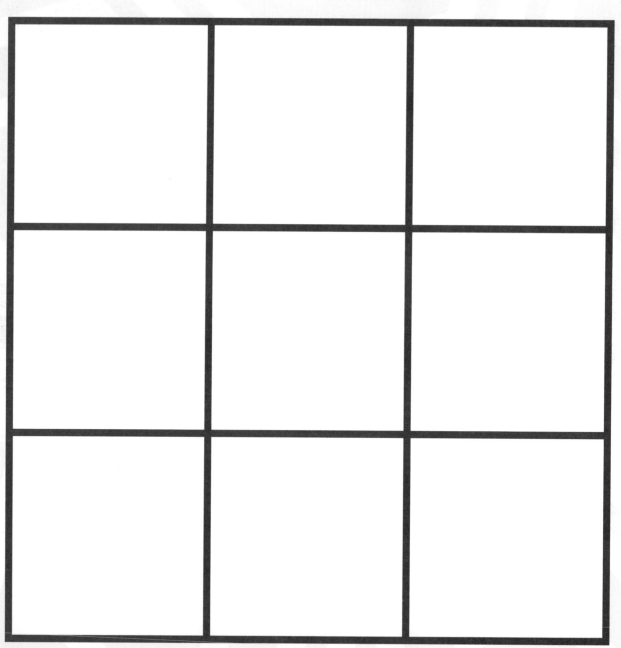

DOT-TO-DOT BACKTRACK

When it all goes wrong – Team Rocket start running in the opposite direction! Trace the numbers backwards to complete this picture showing the cowards beating yet another hasty retreat.

ASH'S NAME GAME

Even when he's hungry and battle-weary, there's only one thing on Ash Ketchum's mind! Fill in the names of these awesome Sinnoh Pokémon and then read down the first letter of each to spell out our hero's dream.

1. ☐☐☐☐☐☐☐☐

2. ☐☐☐☐☐

3. ☐☐☐☐☐☐

4. ☐☐☐☐☐☐☐☐☐☐

5. ☐☐☐☐☐☐

6. ☐☐☐☐☐☐☐☐

7. ☐☐☐☐☐☐☐☐

Need a hand?
Find the Pokédex from the middle pages and stick it in here. Now match the right name to each creature and the answer will appear!

CRAZY COUNTING

Looks like Ash, Dawn and Brock are seriously outnumbered! Count up how many creatures are on the attack and then choose a Pokémon from the sticker sheet who you think has the moves to take them on!

Number of creatures:

BATTLE BLUES

These cool-blue Pokémon are missing the rest of their colours! Use felt-tips or colouring pencils to make each of these Sinnoh stars leap off the page.

RE-LIVING THE LEGEND

Dialga, Palkia and Darkrai loom large in Sinnoh mythology. Dinosaur-like Dialga and Palkia are said to have the power to control space and time, but is mysterious Darkrai friend or foe? Put the sticker shaped jigsaw pieces in the right places to bring these ancient deities to life.

CREEPY CROSS-OUTS

Which fang-baring Pokémon hangs upside down from trees, ready to strike on unsuspecting foes? Cross out all the letters that appear in the grid more than once, then reorder the remaining ones until you spell out the hidden name.

G	K	D	B	W	N	P	T	Q	D
F	J	T	T	E	D	Y	O	H	Y
A	Q	T	J	H	F	W	V	M	T
E	B	U	D	Z	Q	B	K	D	N
J	M	P	V	L	A	X	F	Z	I
S	H	F	E	Y	Z	H	Z	A	Y
F	N	Q	X	V	J	P	M	U	T
D	K	A	H	D	Z	W	R	Q	D
P	E	F	N	J	K	Y	P	F	N
Z	T	A	B	H	C	E	X	A	J

EXTRA CLUE!

Find the sticker that fits over this shadow and the mystery creature will be staring you in the face.

ODD-EVOLUTION-OUT

Dawn's Pokédex is in meltdown! The malfunctioning machine is generating such inaccurate data she doesn't know which evolutions are correct and which are bogus. Can you help her sort things out?

Use your Pokémon expertise to analyse each of the pictures below. Each chain features an evolution that shouldn't be there. Put a cross next to each one as soon as you spot it.

1. FINNEON · GOLDEEN · SEAKING

2. SHIELDON · BASTIODON · GOLEM

3. BUNEARY · BIBAREL · BIDOOF

4. GIBLE · GABITE · RAMPARDOS

A Pokémon is needed to replace the last evolution chain. Stick a picture of it in here!

GARCHOMP

ASH'S ALPHABET

Part 1

There are so many awesome Pokémon to be found on Sinnoh Island – from the dizzy heights of Mount Coronet to the frenetic streets of Jubilife City. Ash wants to meet them all and take them on in battle too if he can!

Use your stickers to help Ash and Pikachu complete this photo album featuring all their favourite Sinnoh Pokémon. Use Ash's notes to help you guess where each picture sticker should go.

A

ABRA
This Psychic Pokèmon spends most of the day asleep!

B

BRONZONG
Not to be underestimated – a Bronzong beat Dawn's Buizel.

C

CROAGUNK
Right from the start, Brock's purple Croagunk followed him everywhere!

D

DUSKNOIR
This curious Ghost-type Pokèmon scares me!

EMPOLEON
Empoleon gave Pikachu a tough battle, but we defeated it in the end!

FROSLASS
This cool customer can freeze people with its icy breath!

GALLADE
Gallade has great manners, but the swords on its elbows pack a mean punch!

HIPPOWDON
This massive Ground-type Pokèmon likes to wallow in deserts and sand basins.

INFERNAPE
When Brock's Croagunk took on Infernape, it moved at lightning speed!

KRICKETUNE
When Kricketune rubs its arms together, it makes interesting music!

LEAFEON
Can you believe that this Pokèmon is just one of Eevee's seven evolutions?

MOTHIM
This Bug Pokèmon is more interested in stealing Combee's honey than battling Trainers!

THE ALPHABET CONCLUDES ON PAGE 32!

RIDDLE ME THIS

The Pokémon team have devised their toughest brain challenge yet! Work your way through the clues in the riddle, writing each letter in the box below.

My first starts Shinx, Skorupi and Shieldon,

My second is in Grotle, and also Gastrodon.

My third is in Beautifly and seconds Buneary,

My fourth sits in Chansey, a creature that's cheery.

My fifth ends Toxicroak, but starts Kadabra,

My last begins the Bug-type, fierce Yanmega.

WHO AM I?

Now stick in a picture of the correct Pokémon!

20

MAKE YOUR OWN POKÉMON STICKERS

This book is packed with an unbelievable collection of Pokémon stickers, but when you've used them all up – it's time to get creative! Brock will show you how to make your own homemade stickers, ready to lick n' stick on books, pictures and cards.

YOU WILL NEED:
- White paper
- Felt-tip pens
- Scissors
- 2 teaspoons powdered gelatine
- 4 teaspoons boiling water
- Cotton bud

1. Draw some Pokémon sticker designs on a sheet of white paper.
2. Cut each one out as accurately as you can, then turn the pictures over so they are laying face down on the table. **TAKE CARE WITH SCISSORS!**
3. Spoon the gelatine into a glass bowl and then ask an adult to pour in the water.
4. Stir the mixture till the gelatine dissolves and then allow it to cool until there is no more steam.
5. Use a cotton bud to lightly dab a thin layer of the gelatine solution onto the back of each cut-out.
6. When all of the designs are completely dry, you're ready to start sticking! Lightly rub a little water on the back of each one and then stick it wherever you like.

I'm going to make some cool Croagunk and Sudowoodo stickers to go on my journal. Which Pokémon are your favourite?

DARK SIDE COLOURING POSTER

Flick through the sticker sheets. Can you find the ghostly picture featuring some of Sinnoh's most intriguing Pokémon? Stick the mini-poster at the bottom of the page, then let this unique clan influence and inspire you to colour in your own amazing artwork!

23

DAWN'S

Before they arrived at the Veilstone City Gym, Dawn never could have predicted that she would challenge Leader Maylene to a Pokémon battle! She sent Buneary and Ambipom in first, before calling on old friend Piplup.

Piplup is ready to combat with Lucario. Can you draw a picture of the determined Pokémon into the scene? Find the right sticker and use it as a colouring guide, then decide what move it is

BATTLE DRAW

STICKER SUDOKU

Virtual Pokémon, Porygon-Z has found this data for your challenge! Use your logic to fill the missing numbers into this maths square. **Every 2 x 2 block must include the figures 1 to 4.**

D&P RULE
The numbers 1 to 4 must only feature once in each block, row or column.

1	2		
3			
4		2	1
		3	

When you've written the numbers in the right places, stick a picture of Porygon-Z here!

ABOMASNOW

ASH

PACHIRISU

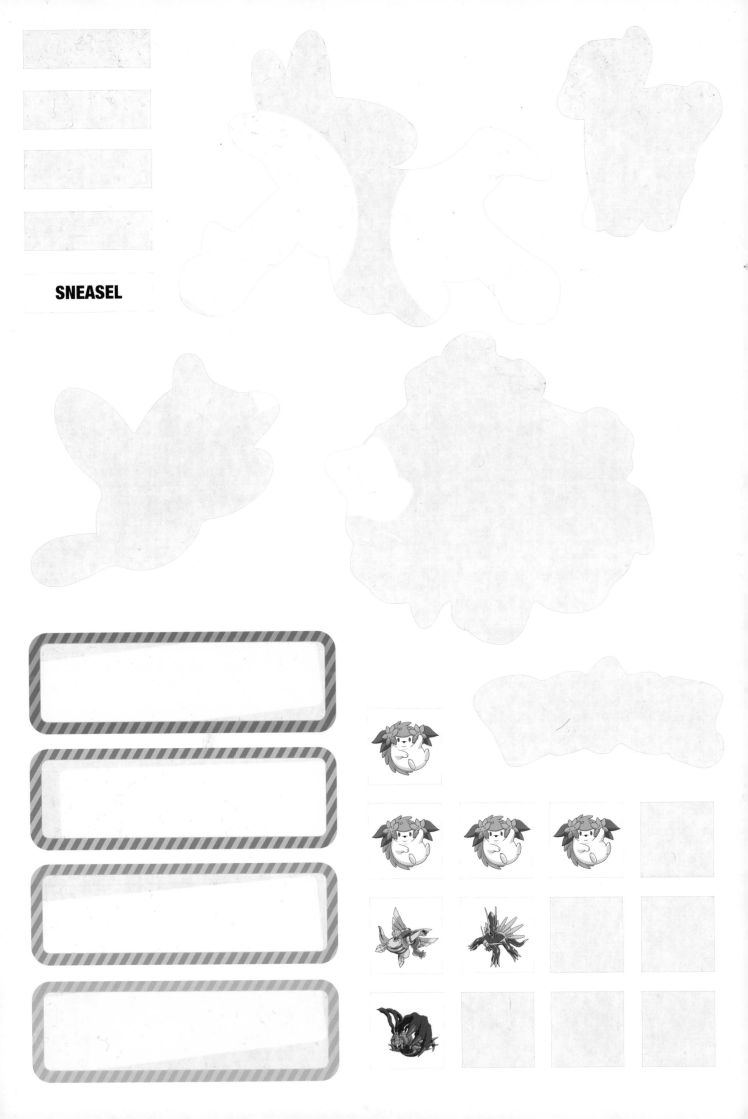

SNEASEL

HAPPINY

0-5
STILL TRAINING!

6-10
POKÉMON FAN

11-15
AWESOME EXPERT

16-20
POKÉMON MASTER

CHINGLING

COLOUR IT! LEAFEON

Use woody shades of brown and green to colour in this Grass-Type Pokémon! Leafeon looks harmless, but its sharp leaf tail can be used to slice and cut.

POKEMON PICTURE QUIZ

It's time to pit your wits against Ash and Pikachu in this multiple choice quiz!

Q1

How many evolutions does Hippopotas have?

A :: 0.............................☐
B :: 2.............................☐
C :: 1.............................☐

Q2

What is the name of Team Rocket's mysterious boss?

A :: Giovanni ....☐
B :: Gianluca ....☐
C :: Antonio ....☐

Q3

This Pokémon possesses the Sand Veil ability, but what is its name?

A :: Cranidos ....☐
B :: Onix...........................☐
C :: Gible..........................☐

Q4

How much food does Munchlax get through every day?

A :: It's own bodyweight.....☐
B :: Five sackfuls...............☐
C :: Only a few mouthfuls..☐

Q5

What is one of the Flying Pokémon's most powerful battle moves?

A :: Bubblebeam ....☐
B :: Brave Bird.................☐
C :: Thunderbolt ....☐

Q6

Floatzel is evolved from which Water-type?

A :: Buizel ....☐
B :: Azumarill ....☐
C :: Magikarp ....☐

Q7

What is this Pokémon's name?

A :: Rotom.......................☐
B :: Bronzong ....☐
C :: Probopass..................☐

Q8

When Wormadam evolved, what happened to its cloak?

A :: It withered and dropped off...☐
B :: Other small Pokémon came to live in it..................................☐
C :: It became part of its body .....☐

Q9

How does Dusknoir use its antenna?

A :: To pick up radio waves from the spirit world ....☐
B :: To conduct electricity ....☐
C :: To fix its helmet in place ....☐

Q10

Who is this Pokémon?

A :: Phione ....☐
B :: Manaphy ....☐
C :: Mantyke ....☐

WALL OF FAME

How did you do? Check your answers, then find the sticker that matches your score and place it here.

COPY

Turtwig, Chimchar, Pikachu and Piplup prove that size doesn't always matter! Each loyal Pokémon is ready to go into battle for Ash and his friends, even if the odds are stacked against them.

Copy the little squares into the blank grid on the right hand page, taking care to draw the squares in alphabetical order. Now colour them!

JUMBLE

A	**B**	**C**
D	**E**	**F**
G	**H**	**I**

ASH'S ALPHABET Part 2

Can you complete Ash's cool Sinnoh photo album, by putting in the missing Pokémon stickers?

N

NOCTOWL
Never take on a Noctowl after dark, its super-strength eyes don't miss a thing!

O

ONIX
Roark's Onix at the Oreburgh City Gym was a force to be reckoned with!

P

PURUGLY
This whiskered brute is evolved from Glameow.

Q

QUAGSIRE
Watch out Pikachu! Quagsire can't be harmed by electricity!

ROTOM
Rotom's plasma body enables it to shrink into TVs and computers!

SHELLOS
The East and West shores of Sinnoh are home to two types of Shellos!

TORTERRA
When a herd of Torterra all walk together, they look like a moving forest.

UXIE
Sinnoh people describe Uxie as the Being of Knowledge.

VESPIQUEN
Approach with caution - this waspish Pokèmon will do anything to protect its colony!

WEAVILE
My rival Paul owns a Weavile, a fearsome opponent in battle.

YANMEGA
I'll never forget when Jessie unleashed a Yanmega against me and my friends!

ZUBAT
In battle, Zubat is able to use Brave Bird!

ELIMINATION GRID

Which new Pokémon is Ash looking up in his Pokédex? Study each clue, then rule out the wrong entries until you get to the right answer!

Cherrim	Ponyta	Starly
Phione	Lucario	Monferno
Piplup	Bronzor	Glaceon

CLUES

1. Its body is a blue colour.
2. It occupies the square below a Fire-Type Pokémon
3. It runs on all fours.

Stick a picture of the correct Pokémon in here!

MEOWTH'S MATHS CODE

Meowth's one smart Pokémon pussycat! He's written a message in code so that only his Team Rocket henchmen can understand him. Solve the sums and then use the key to uncover what's on his mind.

[7+7] [10-3] [9+2] [6+5] [20-5]

___ ___ ___ ___ ___

[6-5] [12+3] [13-2] [8-7] [20+2]

___ ___ ___ ___ ___

[7+4] [16+6] [17-2] [15-4]

___ ___ ___ ___

[12+9] [2+6] [31-6] [14+1] [21-20] [27-5] [3+3] !

___ ___ ___ ___ ___ ___ ___!

One of the letter codes is missing, can you figure out what number represents the letter 'A'? Sticker the answer in below.

A	B	C	D	E	F	G	H	I	J	K	L	M
	9	1	17	8	20	14	22	8	3	25	2	18

N	O	P	Q	R	S	T	U	V	W	X	Y	Z
13	7	21	26	4	23	11	6	16	19	10	5	12

FRIENDS TO THE END!

Ash's belief that Pokémon should be treated with kindness and respect has reaped him huge rewards in the Battle Gym. Stick his most trusted Pokémon friends around him – Pikachu, Chimchar, Turtwig and Aipom.

WATERY
COLOUR-BY-NUMBERS

Sinnoh waters teem with bizarre Pokémon life-forms – from entrancing fish-like species to strange deep sea predators! Use the colour code to bring the scene to life.

MEGA MATCHES

Becoming a Pokémon Trainer is a destiny fulfilled by very few. Do you have what it takes to be one of the lucky ones? Give your Pokémon brain a workout by matching up each of the Pokédex profiles below with the right photo.

Eagle-eyed puzzlers will notice that one of the Pokémon pictures is missing. Find the correct sticker and put it in place.

A.

B.

1. GEODUDE
THE ROCK POKÉMON

GEODUDE IS OFTEN FOUND ON MOUNTAIN ROADS WITH HALF OF ITS BODY BURIED IN THE GROUND, SO IT CAN OBSERVE MOUNTAIN TRAVELLERS.

2. MEDITITE
THE MEDITATE POKÉMON.

MEDITITE USES MEDITATIONS TO INCREASE ITS POWER, NEVER SKIPPING A SINGLE DAY OF YOGA.

C.

3. SHINX
THE FLASH POKÉMON.

WHEN IT SENSES DANGER, THE HAIRS ON ITS BODY LIGHT UP AND IT RUNS AWAY, LEAVING ITS OPPONENT DAZED.

4. AZUMARILL
THE AQUA RABBIT POKÉMON

AZUMARILL LIVES IN RIVERS AND LAKES, AND WHILE IN WATER ITS BODY COLOUR AND PATTERN CONFUSES ITS ENEMIES.

D.

FOREST
HIDE AND SEEK

Brock's Sudowoodo is in trouble, can you help the Breeder track his friend down? Work your way along the woodland paths, colouring the Pokémon that you pass along the way.

GIRATINA AND THE SKY WARRIOR

One Shaymin's life is changed forever when it crosses the path of Giratina, the awesome Ghost Dragon Pokémon! Tell its perilous story by using your stickers to fill in the blanks on the page.

Deep in the heart of the forest

a tiny Pokémon named

stumbled into the midst of an awesome

battle ground. Legendary giants and

were locked in terrible combat, making the earth shake with each

resounding blow. During the battle, found itself pulled

into s mysterious Reverse World, where a poison gas had

been released. used its Seed Flare move to purify the

fumes, before escaping back to Sinnoh.

Later  and his friends ran into . Together

they were pulled back into Reverse World where they learnt

the source of 's fury. The Ghost Dragon Pokémon had

witnessed an epic battle between and that

had polluted its realm with toxic gas. Although had

neutralised the devastating fumes, was bent on

revenge. Now the friends have to find their way back to Sinnoh

before danger crosses their path yet again!

TOTALLY TOXIC!

COLOURING POSTER

When these Poison Pokémon hit town, you can look but you better not touch! Each one has evolved its own unique method of producing venom, some so powerful that even a drop could kill.

Stick the mini-poster in here, then use it to help you pick the right felt-tips or pencils to bring the poster to life.

43

P... P... PIKACHU! WORDSEARCH

Pikachu is not the only Pokémon whose name begins with P – many more roam the mountains and forests on Sinnoh Island.

Stick in the missing picture clues, then try and find the ten Pokémon hiding somewhere in this word grid.

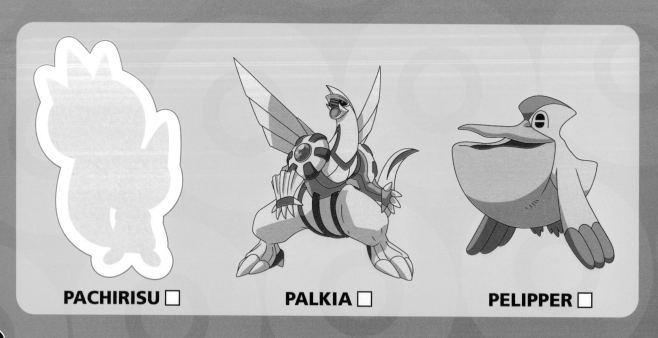

PACHIRISU ☐   **PALKIA** ☐   **PELIPPER** ☐

ONE LAST TIP: The names could be running forwards, backwards, diagonally or upside down!

PICHU ☐   **PIKACHU** ☐   **PIPLUP** ☐

P	E	L	I	P	P	E	R	K	P
I	U	W	P	U	R	U	G	L	Y
P	D	S	A	P	O	N	Y	T	A
L	P	X	I	B	I	Z	O	M	U
U	V	T	K	R	P	P	Y	C	H
P	Q	P	L	K	I	D	H	F	C
A	F	B	A	R	C	H	T	L	A
P	L	X	P	G	H	S	C	J	K
N	P	S	Y	D	U	C	K	A	I
I	E	P	U	L	P	N	I	R	P

PONYTA ☐   **PRINPLUP** ☐   **PSYDUCK** ☐   **PURUGLY** ☐

BROCK'S BUDDIES

Great meals, expert training and a experience in battle make Brock the best Breeder any Pokémon could wish for. Colour in this awesome scene showing some of his favourite Pokémon, then finish it off by sticking in Croagunk at the front.

LOST LINES

Ash has written a letter to his good friend Dawn, can you help her read it? The picture clues will help you piece Ash's story together, word by word. After you fill in each missing word, colour it in.

Dear _____

Yesterday, _____ and I had the most unbelievable adventure! It all began when I headed outside to work on some new battle moves with _____ and _____. Suddenly the sky turned dark, and a huge hot air balloon appeared over the mountain tops in the distance. It was _____ _____ and I had a hunch that they were up to no good.

Within seconds, _____ attacked us from the skies. _____ and I ducked as the Poison moth dived again and again - now it was time for _____ and _____ to get some action! _____ stormed into Brave Bird, while _____ blasted the balloon with an awesome explosion of thunderbolts. There was a giant bang and then, (you guessed it!) _____ were blasting off once again!

See ya soon,

___

CHAINS

A great Trainer is like a detective, sensing the moods and feelings of the Pokémon it encounters. It's time to summon up all your mental powers and deduce which ones are concealed on this page. Crack the clues, then put the right answer sticker at the bottom of each chain.

 — I'm an Electric-type Pokémon — Dawn chooses me as a companion — My fur balls crackle with static electricity

1   HARUSCIPI =

I'm a Grass/Ice-type Pokémon

2

I live on isolated mountain peaks

I can stir up fierce snow blizzards

WOBAMOANS =

I'm a Normal-type Pokémon

3

Brock won me at the Dress-up competition

I love to carry around a white egg-shaped rock

PAYHINP =

I'm an Psychic-type Pokémon

4

I am able to levitate

I make a cry by agitating an orb at the back of my throat

GINNHIGLC =

I'm a Dark/Ice-type Pokémon

5

My claws are razor-sharp

I feed on eggs stolen out of nests

SELNASE =

ANSWERS

SINNOH STICKERS

Page 4 - ASH

1. Pallet Town
2. Ketchum
3. Paul

Page 5 - TEAM ROCKET

1. Giovanni
2. Seviper
3. He can understand all types of speech.

Page 6 - BROCK

1. Pewter City
2. Croagunk
3. Cooking

Page 7 - DAWN

1. Piplup
2. Her mother Johanna
3. Twin Leaf Town

Page 10 - Ash's Name Game

Ash dreams of being a **TRAINER.**

1. **T**ORTERRA
2. **R**OTOM
3. **A**IPOM
4. **I**NFERNAPE
5. **N**OCTOWL
6. **E**MPOLEON
7. **R**OSERADE

Page 11 - Crazy Counting

There are **11 CREATURES**

Pages 14-15 - Re-living the Legend

Page 16 - Creepy Cross-outs

G	K	D	B	W	N	P	T	Q	D
F	J	T	T	E	D	Y	O	H	Y
A	Q	T	J	H	F	W	V	M	T
E	B	U	D	Z	Q	B	K	D	N
J	M	P	V	L	A	X	F	Z	I
S	H	F	E	Y	Z	H	Z	A	Y
F	N	Q	X	V	J	P	M	U	T
D	K	A	H	D	Z	W	R	Q	D
P	E	F	N	J	K	Y	P	F	N
Z	T	A	B	H	C	E	X	A	J

IT'S GLISCOR

Page 17 - Odd-Evolution-Out

1. Finneon
2. Golem
3. Buneary
4. Rampardos

RAMPARDOS should be replaced by **GARCHOMP.**

Pages 18-19 - Ash's Alphabet Part 1

CROAGUNK
Right from the start, Brock's purple Croagunk followed him everywhere!

FROSLASS
This cool customer can freeze people with its icy breath!

LEAFEON
Can you believe that this Pokémon is just one of Eevee's seven evolutions?

Page 20 - Riddle Me This

STUNKY

Page 26 - Sticker Sudoku

1	2	4	3
3	4	1	2
4	3	2	1
1	2	3	4